Animals i...

by Maryellen Gregoire

Nancy E. Harris, M.Ed—Reading
National Reading Consultant

capstone
classroom
Heinemann Raintree • Red Brick Learning
division of Capstone

Many animals live in the forest.

Many animals move in the forest.

I see a bald eagle flying in the sky.

The bald eagle has a white head. It has a yellow beak.

I see a bluebird flying in the sky.

The bluebird has a blue head. It has a black beak.

I see a beaver swimming in the water.

The beaver has a stick house.
It is made with wood.

I see a frog swimming in the water.

The frog has a mud house.
It is made with water.

I see a raccoon hiding in the forest.

The raccoon has seeds.
It has walnuts.

I see a rabbit hiding in the forest.

The rabbit has plants.
It has grass.

How does a deer move in the forest?